ABOUT THE BANK STREET READY-TO-READ SERIES

Seventy years of educational research and innovative teaching have given the Bank Street College of Education the reputation as America's most trusted name in early childhood education.

Because no two children are exactly alike in their development, we have designed the *Bank Street Ready-to-Read* series in three levels to accommodate the individual stages of reading readiness of children ages four through eight.

- ◉ *Level 1:* GETTING READY TO READ—read-alouds for children who are taking their first steps toward reading.
- ● *Level 2:* READING TOGETHER—for children who are just beginning to read by themselves but may need a little help.
- ○ *Level 3:* I CAN READ IT MYSELF—for children who can read independently.

Our three levels make it easy to select the books most appropriate for a child's development and enable him or her to grow with the series step by step. The *Bank Street Ready-to-Read* books also overlap and reinforce each other, further encouraging the reading process.

We feel that making reading fun and enjoyable is the single most important thing that you can do to help children become good readers. And we hope you'll be a part of Bank Street's long tradition of learning through sharing.

The Bank Street
College of Education

To Karen
—B.B.

To Agnès T.
—V.M.

YOU ARE MUCH TOO SMALL
A Bantam Little Rooster Book
Simultaneous paper-over-board and trade paper editions/September 1990

Little Rooster is a trademark of Bantam Books,
a division of Bantam Doubleday Dell Publishing Group, Inc.

Series graphic design by Alex Jay/Studio J
Associate Editor: Gillian Bucky
Special thanks to James A. Levine, Betsy Gould,
Erin B. Gathrid, and Gwendolyn Dunaif.

Library of Congress Cataloging-in-Publication Data

Boegehold, Betty Virginia Doyle.
You are much too small / by Betty Boegehold ;
illustrated by Valérie Michaut.
p. cm. — (Bank Street ready-to-read)
"A Byron Preiss book."
"A Bantam little rooster book."
Summary: Too small to help family members
with their chores, Totty Pig surprises
everyone by building a tent.
ISBN 0-553-05895-9. — ISBN 0-553-34925-2 (pbk.)
[1. Size—Fiction. 2. Pigs—Fiction.]
I. Michaut, Valérie. ill. II. Title. III. Series
PZ7.B6337Yo
[E]—dc20

89-18208   CIP   AC

Published simultaneously in the United States and Canada

Bantam Books are published by Bantam Books, a division of Bantam Doubleday
Dell Publishing Group, Inc. Its trademark, consisting of the words "Bantam Books"
and the portrayal of a rooster, is Registered in U.S. Patent and Trademark Office
and in other countries. Marca Registrada. Bantam Books, 666 Fifth Avenue, New
York, New York 10103.

PRINTED IN THE UNITED STATES OF AMERICA

0 9 8 7 6 5 4 3 2 1

Bank Street Ready-to-Read™

You Are Much Too Small

by Betty D. Boegehold
Illustrated by Valérie Michaut

A Byron Preiss Book

A BANTAM LITTLE ROOSTER BOOK
NEW YORK · TORONTO · LONDON · SYDNEY · AUCKLAND

All the pigs were busy.
All the pigs but Totty Pig.

Tritty-trot-trot, tritty-trot-trot.
Totty Pig went into the kitchen.
Father Pig was making flip cakes.
He flipped them into the air
and caught them in a pan.
Flip! Flip! Flip!

"May I help flip the cakes?"
asked Totty Pig.
"Oh, no, Totty Pig," said Father Pig,
"you are much too small."

Tritty-trot-trot, tritty-trot-trot.
Totty Pig went upstairs.
Mother Pig was building a shelf.
Drill! Drill! Drill!

"May I help build the shelf?"
asked Totty Pig.
"Oh, no, Totty Pig," said Mother Pig,
"you are much too small."

Tritty-trot-trot, tritty-trot-trot.
Totty Pig went down the stairs.
Grandpa Pig was setting the clock.
Ding-dong! Ding-dong!

"May I help set the clock?"
asked Totty Pig.
"Oh, no, Totty Pig," said Grandpa Pig,
"you are much too small."

Tritty-trot-trot, tritty-trot-trot.
Totty Pig went outdoors.
Sister Pig was cutting the grass.
Cut! Cut! Cut!

"May I help cut the grass?"
asked Totty Pig.
"Oh, no, Totty Pig," said Sister Pig,
"you are much too small."

Totty Pig was sad.
She said to herself,
"I am too small to help anyone.
I will go live by myself."

So Totty Pig went to the toolshed.
She found an old blanket
and some rope.

Tritty-trot-trot, tritty-trot-trot.
Totty Pig went down the road.
"I will make a tent," she said.
"A little tent, just right for me."

Soon Father Pig called,
"Totty Pig, Totty Pig, I need you!
Come taste my flip cakes."

Mother Pig called,
"Totty Pig, Totty Pig, I need you!
Come put your books on the shelf."

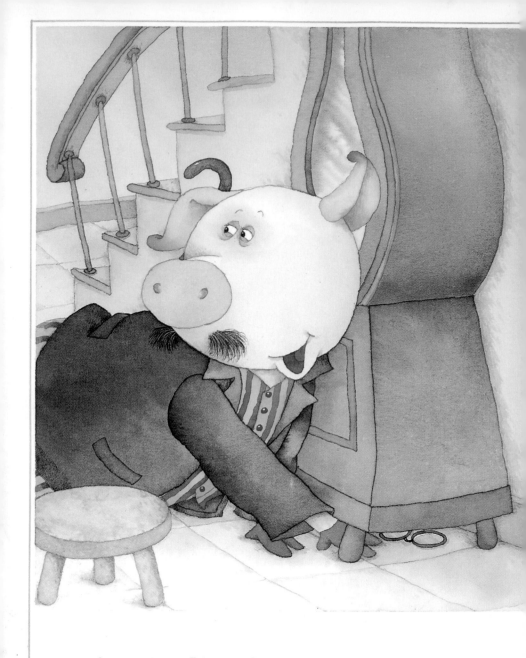

Grandpa Pig called,
"Totty Pig, Totty Pig, I need you!
Come help find my glasses."

Sister Pig called,
"Totty Pig, Totty Pig, I need you!
Come help me rake the grass."

But Totty Pig didn't come.
All the pigs asked,
"Where is Totty Pig?"
They looked inside the house.
They looked outside the house.
But they couldn't find Totty Pig.

"We must find Totty Pig,"
they all cried.
Tritty-trot-trot, tritty-trot-trot.
They ran down the road.
Under a tree they saw a little tent.

Totty Pig was inside.
"Oh, Totty," they cried.
"We've found you.
Please come home now.
We need you to help us."

The pigs stuck their heads
into the tent.
"What a nice house
you have made," they said.
"Can we come inside?"
"Oh, no," said Totty Pig.
"I am much too small to help.
But you are much too big
for this tent."

"Oh, Totty, please come out,"
begged Mother Pig.
"Totty, please come home,"
begged Father Pig.

But Totty Pig stayed right in her tent.
So all the pigs sat down outside
and cried, "Sniff, grunt. Sniff, grunt."

At last Totty Pig said,
"Stop sniffing and grunting.
If you really need me,
I will come back.
But when I feel like being
by myself, I will come here."

Totty Pig came out of her tent.
And she led the pigs back
up the road and all the way
to the pig house.

Tritty-trot-trot, tritty-trot-trot.